SPACE PENGUINS

METEOR MADNESS!

For Tamara Clover ~ **L A C**

For Josh ~ **J D**

STRIPES PUBLISHING
An imprint of Little Tiger Press
1 The Coda Centre, 189 Munster Road,
London SW6 6AW

A paperback original
First published in Great Britain in 2013

ISBN: 978-1-84715-393-7

Printed and bound in the UK.

10 9 8 7 6 5 4 3 2 1

METEOR MADNESS!

L A COURTENAY

ILLUSTRATED BY
JAMES DAVIES

MEET THE
SPACE
PENGUINS...

CAPTAIN:
Captain T. Krill
Emperor penguin
Height: 1.10m
Looks: yellow ear patches and
noble bearing
Likes: swordfish minus the
sword
Lab tests: showed leadership
qualities in fish challenge
Guaranteed to: keep calm in
a crisis

**FIRST MATE (ONCE UPON
A TIME):**
Beaky Wader, now known as
Dark Wader
Once Emperor penguin, now
part-robot
Height: 1.22m
Looks: shiny black armour
and evil laugh
Likes: prawn pizzas and ruling
the universe
Lab tests: cheated at every
challenge
Guaranteed to: cause trouble

PILOT (WITH NO SENSE OF DIRECTION):

Rocky Waddle
Rockhopper penguin
Height: 45cm
Looks: long yellow eyebrows
Likes: mackerel ice cream
Lab tests: fastest slider
in toboggan challenge
Guaranteed to: speed through
an asteroid belt while reading
charts upside down

SECURITY OFFICER AND HEAD CHEF:

Fuzz Allgrin
Little Blue penguin
Height: 33cm
Looks: small with fuzzy blue
feathers
Likes: fish fingers in cream and
truffle sauce
Lab tests: showed creativity
and aggression in ice-carving
challenge
Guaranteed to: defend ship,
crew and kitchen with his life

SHIP'S ENGINEER:

Splash Gordon
King penguin
Height: 95cm
Looks: orange ears and chest
markings
Likes: squid
Lab tests: solved ice-cube
challenge in under four
seconds
Guaranteed to: fix anything

LOADING...

I am ICEcube and you are on board the *Tunafish*, the coolest spaceship in the universe. It's cool because it's full of penguins, and penguins like to keep the temperature down. I'm the *Tunafish*'s onboard computer and I can't tell lies, so you know that this is true.

Yes. Penguin astronauts fly the *Tunafish*. As penguins don't normally fly, and have never been to space before, this is unusual. But NASA decided that penguin astronauts could send useful information about space back to Earth. They trained five penguins, gave them spacesuits and blasted them into orbit. One disappeared to make plans for ruling the universe by himself. The rest lost contact with Earth, and now have only my very large brain to keep them company out here among the stars.

My database says: NASA are a bunch of turnip-heads.

It's a shame that the penguins got lost, because we have learned a lot about space that we could share with Earth.

Fuzz Allgrin invented a nice pickle using Massive Bugle-blasting Blagwit bogies.

Captain T. Krill learned that being brave is all very well, until you upset a Massive Bugle-blasting Blagwit by picking its nose.

Rocky Waddle recently found out that left and right are not the same thing, except when you're on the planet Mirramirra.

And Splash Gordon has learned not to have a birthday party when space pirates are attacking the *Tunafish*.

RECALCULATING…

Sorry, Splash hasn't learned this yet. The crew are throwing him a birthday party right now, singing rude songs about seals and eating too much. I have been trying to tell them about the space pirates for four minutes and twenty-three seconds, but no one is listening.

The space pirates will arrive in approximately twelve minutes and forty seconds. So will the birthday cake. In the meantime, I hope the *Tunafish* crew enjoy Fuzz's piranha biscuits. They won't make the space pirates go away, but they make a lovely SNAP when you bite into them.

Yum yum. Enjoy them while you can.

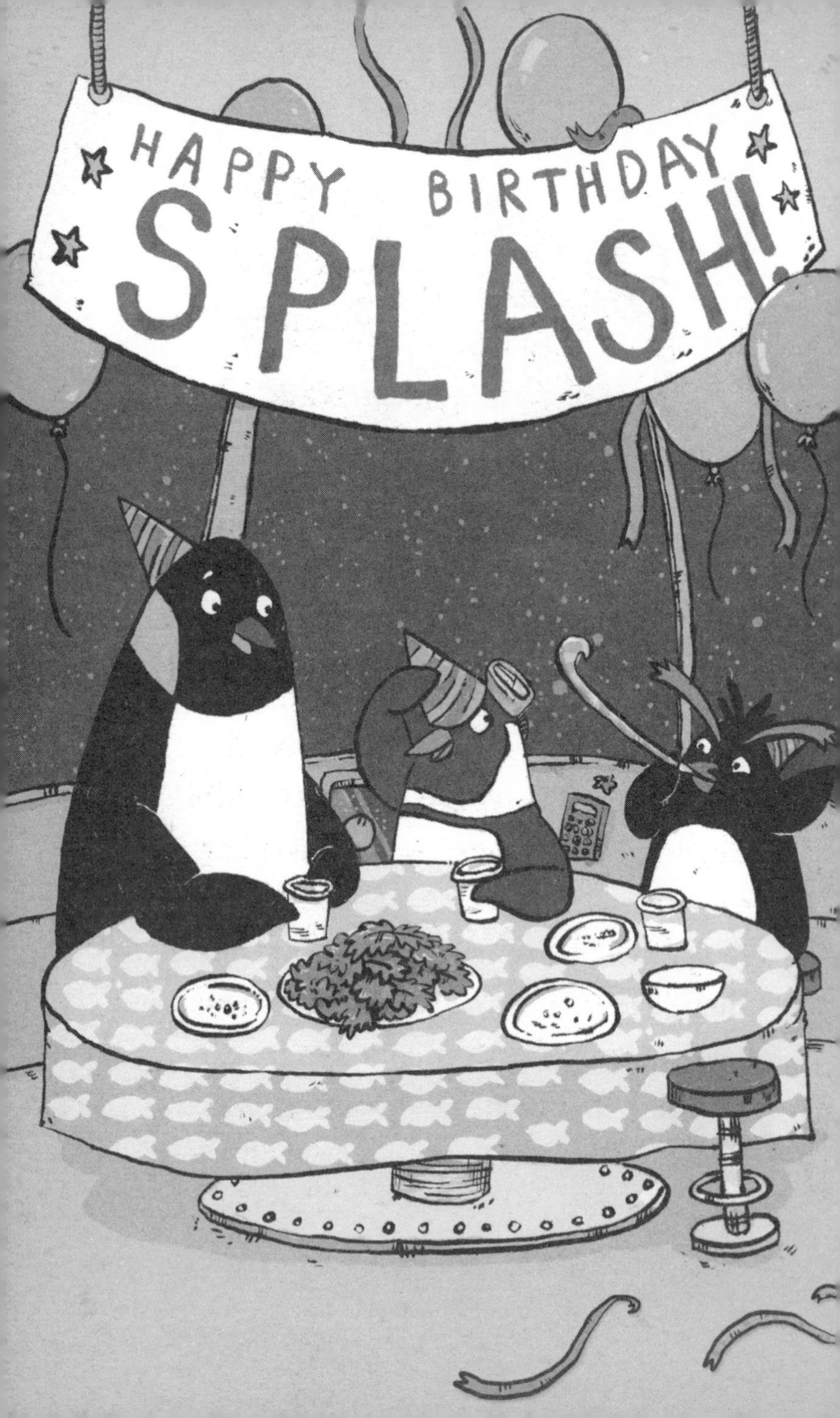
HAPPY BIRTHDAY
SPLASH!

CHAPTER ONE

HAPPY BIRTHDAY SPLASH!

Balloons and streamers littered the cabin floor of the spaceship *Tunafish*. A large banner saying HAPPY BIRTHDAY SPLASH! hung overhead as three penguins in party hats sat round a decorated party table, happily resting their flippers on their full bellies. The *Tunafish* cruised along in autopilot.

"Sing that song about seals again, Rocky!" said Splash Gordon, the Ship's Engineer. His party hat had fallen over his eyes and made him look like he had two beaks.

The *Tunafish*'s pilot, Rocky Waddle, swept his long yellow eyebrows out of his eyes, parped on his party-blower and started singing:

"OH, seals are fat, seals are smelly,
Seals aren't cute like they are on the telly.
We don't like seals, coz they think we're yum,
If we saw a seal in space, we'd kick it up the—"

"THANK YOU, Rocky," said Captain Krill with a frown on his yellow-striped face. "Can you check the flight instruments? I thought I heard a strange pinging noise coming from the autopilot."

Rocky parped on his party-blower again and waddled over to the flight deck. "All knobs, dials and flashing lights on the autopilot are working perfectly, Captain," he reported. "The pinging noise must be coming from somewhere else."

A small fluffy penguin in a large chef's hat came out of the kitchen.

"The pinging sound is Splash's birthday cake," Fuzz Allgrin said, wiping a blob of cake mix off his face.

"My cake is pinging?" asked Splash.

"The oven is pinging," Fuzz said, "to let me know the cake is ready."

"Calling all Space Penguins," said ICEcube, for the fifth time in five minutes.

"We're having a party, ICEcube," Rocky said, waving his flippers around. "Stop doing your bossy voice."

"ICEcube doesn't have a bossy voice," said ICEcube.

"I'm sorry, but you definitely do," said Fuzz.

"Let's talk after the cake, ICEcube," said Captain Krill.

"It's important, Captain," said ICEcube.

"So's my cake," said Splash. "What flavour is it, Fuzz? Sprat? Kipper?"

Fuzz wagged a flour-covered flipper. "You'll have to wait and see, birthday bird. And you have to eat your space-spinach first."

The Space Penguins looked at the party table. All the piranha biscuits, stellar-salmon sandwiches and meteor-mackerel ice cream had gone. The only food left was a large plate of something dark blue and squishy-looking.

"I don't like space-spinach," Splash moaned.

"Me neither," Rocky groaned.

"It must be very good for us," said Captain Krill, "because it tastes terrible."

"Space-spinach is full of vitamins!" Fuzz said. "Who knows when we'll next find a planet where we can go fishing for proper penguin food?"

"Vegetables are BAD for penguins," said Rocky. "We're from the fishy oceans of Antarctica, not a stinky space allotment."

"We're not from Antarctica," Splash said. "We're from the zoo."

"And did they feed us on vegetables in the zoo?" Rocky demanded. "No."

Fuzz folded his flippers. "If you don't eat it, I'll put the cake straight into the waste-disposal chute and fire it into space."

"You wouldn't," gasped Splash.

Fuzz narrowed his eyes. "Watch me."

To set an example to his crew, Captain Krill ate a very small piece of space-spinach and drank a very big glass of iced water. Rocky and Splash nibbled a couple of leaves.

"Very good," said Fuzz. "Now why don't you all play Hide and Beak while I ice the cake?"

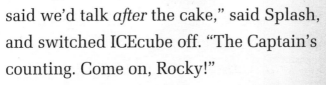

"One, two, three, four…" Captain Krill began, covering his eyes with his flippers.

"Calling all Space Penguins," said ICEcube.

"Captain Krill said we'd talk *after* the cake," said Splash, and switched ICEcube off. "The Captain's counting. Come on, Rocky!"

During their years in space, the Space Penguins had got very good at Hide and Beak. Splash and Rocky rushed away to hide as Fuzz went back into the kitchen.

"…seven, eight, nine, TEN. Coming, ready or not," said Captain Krill. "Make a noise!"

"YOU HAVE TO LOOK FOR US FIRST!" Rocky yelled from the freezing-fog room.

SPACE PENGUINS

Although the *Tunafish* looked small from the outside, it was very spacious with plenty of good hiding places. There were sleeping quarters, a kitchen, an extra-cold store down in the hold, an engine room, a freezing-fog room where the Space Penguins liked to chill out, plenty of big cupboards, a slushy vending machine, a large ice-bath and a room with a wing-pong table.

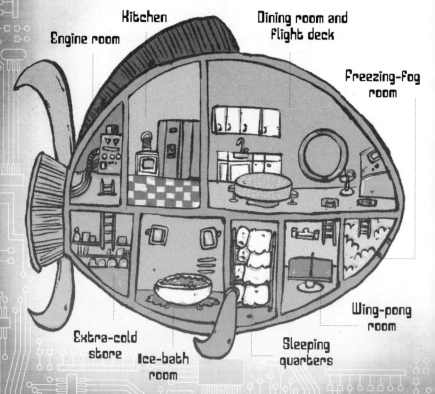

Kitchen

Dining room and flight deck

Engine room

Freezing-fog room

Wing-pong room

Extra-cold store

Ice-bath room

Sleeping quarters

After ten minutes of looking, Captain Krill shouted, "I give up!"

Rocky popped his head out of the freezing-fog room.

"I'm sure I looked in there," said the Captain, frowning.

"Not hard enough, Captain," said Rocky with a smirk.

Splash popped up from underneath the table as Fuzz waddled out of the kitchen with a huge fish-shaped cake covered in glittery grey icing and topped with candles. "A supernova sardine cake!" he gasped. "Just what I wanted! Are you sure you didn't borrow the mind-reading hat I invented last week, Fuzz?"

Splash rubbed his flippers together, admiring his cake.

"Who turned ICEcube off?" Captain Krill asked, noticing that the *Tunafish*'s computer was quiet and dark.

There was a stony silence. Splash looked down guiltily.

"No harm done," said Captain Krill, switching ICEcube back on again. "I hope."

"*Happy Birthday to you,*" the Space Penguins started singing to Splash, "*sushi takeout for two. You look like an orca, but you smell like a—*"

"Red alert," said ICEcube. "Space pirates attacking. Action stations!"

CHAPTER TWO

A NASTY PRESENT

"Bouncing barracudas!" Captain Krill gasped. "Space pirates?"

Space pirates were ruthless and cunning outlaws who cruised around looking for spaceships to capture and treasure to steal. They showed no mercy to prisoners. Every spaceship in the universe was terrified of a space-pirate attack.

The Space Penguins rushed to the window. At first, they couldn't see anything.

Then, suddenly, they saw a fleet of black spaceships. The fleet's perfect blackness made it look as if someone had cut a lot of spaceship-shaped holes out of the starry universe.

"There are dozens of them!" said Captain Krill.

"Sneaky little kippers," said Fuzz. "How dare they interrupt my cake!"

"It's *my* cake, Fuzz," said Splash.

"We haven't even cut it yet!" Fuzz went on. "Don't they realize that this is a birthday party? That's just rude!"

A beam of light blazed at the Space Penguins, dazzling them.

WHOOSH!

Something whizzed past the windscreen of the *Tunafish*, as dark and ripply as a black octopus.

"Time to get out of here," said Rocky.

WHOOSH!

Rocky jumped into the pilot's chair as another something whizzed at the *Tunafish*. Grabbing the controls, he spun the ship around. More jet-black spacecraft were waiting behind them.

"PARTY POOPERS!" Fuzz shouted.

"We're surrounded!" said Splash.

"What now, Captain?" asked Rocky.

"Straight up?" Captain Krill suggested.

Rocky walloped a button. The *Tunafish* rocketed upwards like a crazy elevator. It went so fast that the Space Penguins and the birthday cake were flung to the floor.

"My beautiful supernova sardine cake!" cried Fuzz, struggling to his feet.

"*My* beautiful supernova sardine cake!" shouted Splash.

"It's a flatfish cake now," said Captain Krill sadly.

WHOOSH!

Another ripple through the air. The jet-black attackers were fast. Four of them shot after the *Tunafish*, blocking the penguins' escape. Rocky flipped the little ship like a lucky coin and rocketed back down again. Cake flew everywhere.

The space pirates were closing in, trapping the *Tunafish* like a sprat in a great black net. Rocky revved the engines, but they sounded sluggish.

"Come on," Rocky muttered, revving again.

JUDDER-JUDDER-JUDDER went the engines. The *Tunafish* didn't move. The pirates crowded in a little closer.

"What's wrong?" asked Captain Krill. "Why aren't we moving?"

"I don't know!" said Rocky. "It feels like we're stuck in space glue."

"There must be a problem with the engines," said Splash. He took off his party hat and pulled down his goggles. "I'll go and investigate."

WHOOSH!

"What is that whooshing noise?" said Captain Krill, as Splash headed for the engine room. He looked around the cabin. "I've heard it four times now."

"Well, nothing's hit us," said Rocky. He revved the engines again. With a sudden roar, they flamed powerfully back to life.

"Splash is a genius!" exclaimed Fuzz.

Rocky pressed hard on the thruster. The *Tunafish* whipped towards the surrounding starships at full speed. Fuzz and Captain Krill flung their flippers round the nearest chairs and hung on with their feet flying out behind them.

"What are you doing, Rocky?" gasped Captain Krill. "We're going to crash right into them!"

"I'm playing a game called Chicken," said Rocky, as the spaceship gained speed. "We're going to see who swerves first."

"That's my favourite game," said Fuzz.

The *Tunafish* streaked fearlessly towards the black starships, hanging still and silent in front of them like a massive black wall.

"They're not going anywhere, Rocky!"
said Captain Krill.

Rocky accelerated again. "They will."

"Galloping groupers!" shrieked Fuzz.
"Show them who's boss, Rocky! We're the
Space Penguins, hear us FLAP!"

They could see nothing but the noses
of the starships in front of them now.
Captain Krill closed his eyes and prepared
to be smashed into tiny penguin pieces.

Then the *Tunafish* suddenly tilted on
to its side, squeezed through a tiny gap
between the enemy ships and shot to
freedom on the other side.

CHAPTER THREE

THIS SHIP NEEDS REFUELLING

"I think we lost them," Rocky said breathlessly.

"That was a brave piece of flying," Captain Krill panted.

"Thank you, Captain."

"But we swerved first!" Fuzz complained. "That makes *us* the chickens! The Fuzzmeister is not a chicken. He's a penguin!"

"We didn't swerve," said Rocky. "We just turned sideways a bit and squeezed through a gap."

"We swerved," insisted Fuzz.

"I think they did move away from us, just a bit," said Captain Krill in a soothing voice. "And at least they're not following us now. How about some cake to celebrate the fact that we're still alive?"

The cake lay in sad squishy piles around the cabin of the *Tunafish*. Glittery grey icing glooped from the ceiling. As the Space Penguins helped themselves, their terror of the space pirates began to fade.

Splash reappeared from the engine room. He looked at his cake-eating space mates with a blank expression.

"Splash!" said Rocky, wiping his mouth guiltily. "We couldn't wait. You don't mind, do you?"

Splash turned his eyes on Captain Krill.

"Sugar is good for shock," Captain Krill explained. "Thanks to Rocky's expert flying, we just had a very narrow escape from the pirates."

"You mean the pirates had a very narrow escape from *us*," corrected Fuzz. Icing hung off his beak like a sticky grey beard. "There's a bit of cake left under the table, Splash. It's a mess but it still tastes fantastic, even if I say so myself."

Splash went towards a splattery heap of space-spinach in one corner of the cabin and scooped up a beakful. Gobbling it down, he fixed the others with a nasty glare.

"Did you mean to eat that?" Fuzz said in shock.

"This ship needs refuelling," said Splash in a flat voice.

Rocky frowned. "That's not what the instruments say."

"This ship needs refuelling," Splash repeated.

Rocky hopped out of the pilot's chair. "Show me the fuel gauges in the engine room," he said.

Captain Krill watched his ship's engineer and his pilot head for the engine room with a strange feeling in his tummy.

"Now I've seen everything," said Fuzz. "Splash eating space-spinach instead of cake?" Shaking his head, he fetched a mop and a brush and started to clean up the mess.

"Do you think Splash is OK?" Captain Krill asked.

"He'll be healthier than a freshwater salmon after all that space-spinach," said Fuzz. "Lend a flipper with that duster, will you, Captain?"

Fuzz and Captain Krill worked together to tidy up the birthday mess, loading the astrodynamic dishwasher, scrubbing the *Tunafish*'s metal floor, polishing the rivets in the ceiling and the walls, and putting the leftover food into the waste-disposal chute. Soon the cabin was gleaming like it had been through a cosmic carwash.

"Good job, Fuzz," Captain Krill said, looking around the cabin. "Tidy ship,

tidy mind. Astronauts need tidy minds.
It helps us to think more clearly in our
dangerous space environment."

"My tidy mind thinks Splash and
Rocky are taking a long time in that engine
room," Fuzz said, putting the mop away.
"Perhaps one of us should check on them."

The doors slid open.

"There you are!" said Captain Krill,
as Splash and Rocky entered the cabin
together. "Anything to report?"

"This ship needs refuelling," said Rocky.

"This ship needs refuelling," said Splash.

"It sounds like this ship needs refuelling, Captain," said Fuzz.

Captain Krill sighed. "Fine, we'll dock as soon as we can and refuel. ICEcube, is the next planet a friendly one?"

"The planet Kroesus," said ICEcube. "Population: four billion. Known primarily for its spacetanium mines, Kroesus produces more than three-quarters of the spacetanium supply in the entire universe. Spacetanium is the strongest, lightest metal in the cosmos and is very valuable. Kroesus was robbed ten thousand times a year until it created a unique security system to protect itself from pirates. Its inhabitants are small, yellow and unfriendly."

"If I'd been robbed ten thousand times

a year, I'd be unfriendly, too," said Captain Krill.

"What sort of unique security system?" asked Fuzz.

"Mechanical meteors orbit the planet at twenty thousand kilometres an hour," ICEcube replied. "Every visitor to Kroesus must pass a series of security checks. If the security checks are satisfactory, the meteors are frozen in mid-air and ships can land safely. If the visitors fail the security checks, the meteors burst into flames, setting fire to their ships."

"This ship needs refuelling," said Splash.

"This ship needs refuelling," said Rocky.

"We heard you the first time," said Captain Krill. "Set the coordinates for Kroesus, Rocky. And I really hope we're not pelted with mechanical meteors today."

CHAPTER FOUR

SPACE-SPINACH SANDWICH

Rocky settled down at the controls. "Destination: planet Kroesus," he said, setting the coordinates. "Estimated duration of flight: three hours."

"Estimated time of arrival: twenty-five hundred hours, Kroesus time," said Splash. "Check."

Captain Krill watched his ship's engineer and his pilot. He couldn't put his flipper on it, but something strange was going on.

"Everything OK, guys?" he asked.

Rocky kept his eyes trained on the flight instruments. Splash looked at Captain Krill without twanging up his goggles.

"Dinner!" Fuzz shouted, bringing out a large plate of freshly defrosted space-spinach and a selection of fish sandwiches. "Sorry it's only sandwiches, but we did just have a massive birthday tea."

"Destination: planet Kroesus," said Rocky, not moving.

"Estimated duration of flight: two hours and fifty-nine minutes," added Splash.

"Estimated time of arrival: twenty-five hundred hours, Kroesus time," said Rocky.

"Check," said Splash.

Fuzz set the sandwiches down as Captain Krill took his place at the table. Then Fuzz waddled over to Rocky and Splash with his flippers on his hips. "I said, DINNER!"

The little blue penguin shouted so loudly that a couple of red flashing lights on the flight deck started flashing a bit faster.

"This ship needs refuelling," Rocky and Splash said together.

"So do you, you daft dolphins. Get to that table at once, unless you want a kung-fu chop in the guts from the Fuzzmeister!"

Rocky and Splash turned away from the controls and waddled towards the table. They were moving strangely, as if they'd forgotten how their bodies worked.

"Who's for a sandwich?" said Captain Krill, as Rocky and Splash sat down.

"Space-spinach first," Fuzz interrupted. "And don't complain. It's good for you and—"

Rocky and Splash both shot out their flippers. They scooped up so much space-spinach that there was none left for the

Captain or Fuzz. Splash tipped the whole lot straight into his mouth. Rocky pulled a sandwich apart, took out the fish that was sitting inside and replaced it with a lump of space-spinach. Then he put the bread back together again. Blue space-spinach juice oozed out of the sandwich and dribbled down Rocky's front as he munched it up.

"That is the most disgusting thing I've ever seen," said Fuzz. He gazed at the fish, lying abandoned on the table. "What's the matter with you both?"

"Is there any more space-spinach, Fuzz?" said Captain Krill.

"Not you as well, Captain!" Fuzz gasped. "You're supposed to eat space-spinach, but you're not supposed to LIKE it!"

"I don't like it," Captain Krill assured his chef. "But I'm prepared to do my duty and eat it. And there's none left."

Splash was now wiping the empty plate with his flipper, then putting his flipper in his beak.

"I'll fetch some more from the extra-cold store," Fuzz said. Firing a confused look at Rocky and Splash, he waddled out of the cabin.

"Destination: planet Kroesus," said Rocky, heading back to the flight deck. "Estimated duration of flight: two hours and forty-three minutes. Estimated time of arrival: twenty-five hundred hours, Kroesus time."

"Check," said Splash, waddling after him.

Captain Krill ate a solar-sprat sandwich thoughtfully.

Fuzz headed deep into the belly of the *Tunafish*. Thanks to NASA, the extra-cold store held spare supplies of pretty much everything, from spacesuits to salmon pâté.

"Eating space-spinach," Fuzz muttered to himself. "Enjoying space-spinach. GUZZLING space-spinach. I can't believe I'm fetching more of the stuff. I thought it'd take months to go through the last lot."

He flipped open the hatch to the extra-cold store, enjoying the chilly blast as it ruffled through his feathers.

"Space-spinach," he said thoughtfully to himself, looking around the extra-cold store. "Where did I put it?"

His eyes swept past jars of pickled space-squid, tins of star-whale blubber, flipper brushes, oxygen tanks, ice cubes, boxes of wing-pong balls, bottles of feather conditioner and two pairs of penguin feet, pointing straight up at the ceiling.

"Big beluga bottoms, NASA," Fuzz said out loud, staring at the feet in surprise. "I know you packed spare supplies of everything, but when are we going to need those?"

Fuzz heard the door slide open. His eyes widened as he took in the shadowy stranger in front of him. Then an extra layer of coldness stole over him and everything went black.

CHAPTER FIVE

OOH, THAT'S COLD

Captain Krill was about to go and investigate where Fuzz had got to when the little blue penguin came back into the cabin. He was carrying so much frozen space-spinach that he could hardly see where he was going.

"Destination: planet Kroesus," said Rocky from the flight deck. "Estimated duration of flight: two hours and thirty-one minutes."

"Estimated time of arrival: twenty-five

hundred hours, Kroesus time," said Splash.

Captain Krill followed Fuzz into the kitchen.

"Thank goodness you're back, Fuzz," he said. "There is something seriously wrong with Splash and Rocky. It's all 'destination' this, 'estimated time of arrival' that. If I hear how long we've got to go until we reach Kroesus one more time, I might go mad."

"This ship needs refuelling," said Fuzz, putting the space-spinach away in the kitchen's freezer compartment.

"Believe me, I know that," said Captain Krill. "I think their behaviour has something to do with those pirates. Don't you think it's odd that the pirates attacked us, but then went off again without robbing us or stealing our ship?"

Fuzz took a lump of frozen space-spinach and popped it into his beak. There was a crunching sound as he chewed it up.

"Taste better frozen, does it?" asked Captain Krill. "It can't taste much worse. Listen, Fuzz – we have to do something. Why didn't Splash want any birthday cake? Why did Rocky change his mind like that about us needing fuel? And our destination – Kroesus – is bothering me for some reason. I'm sure that the answer to all this is right under my beak. I just have to look a bit harder."

Captain Krill suddenly clapped his flippers together. "I know! I'll go down to the engine room to see for myself just how much fuel we've got left. I don't mean to say that I don't trust Rocky and Splash, but—" He stopped and smoothed back his yellow ear patches. "OK," he said, "I don't trust Rocky and Splash. But I'll trust my own eyes. If we're really out of fuel, then I'll put their peculiar behaviour down to a simple case of space sickness."

Leaving Fuzz to put away the rest of the space-spinach, Captain Krill waddled back into the cabin.

"Destination: planet Kroesus," said Rocky.

"Estimated duration of flight: two hours and twenty-five minutes," said Splash.

"Don't tell me," said Captain Krill irritably. "Estimated time of arrival: twenty-five hundred hours, Kroesus time?"

"Check," said Splash.

Did they really need to be heading

for this Kroesus place, with its endless spacetanium mines and its deadly mechanical meteor defence system? Captain Krill wondered, waddling towards the engine room as fast as he could. What if they didn't pass the security checks? They'd be blown out of the sky.

He opened the doors. The engines rumbled loudly around him as he headed for the fuel gauges.

LOW said one. VERY LOW said another.

Captain Krill felt guilty. He and his *Tunafish* crew had been through a lot during their time in space. Why was he doubting the loyalty of his pilot and his ship's engineer like this?

NOT LOW AT ALL, said the third.

PRACTICALLY FULL, said the fourth.

WHY ARE YOU CHECKING THE FUEL GAUGES? said the fifth and final one. WE'RE FINE FOR ANOTHER HALF A MILLION LIGHT YEARS. YOU DO YOUR JOB AND WE'LL DO OURS.

Captain Krill gasped. He was right! There *was* something fishy going on. And it wasn't Fuzz's solar-sprat sandwiches!

A cold breeze blew over the Captain's feet. He turned round.

A smoky, dog-like creature stood in front of him on its hind legs. It had a long black snout, short black fur and eyes that didn't reflect any light. It was so black that

the Captain wondered if he was looking
at a shadow.

The creature shimmered in the air.
Captain Krill backed up against the fuel
gauges as it floated towards him.

"Ooh, that's cold," he said, as the
smoke crept over his toes.

It was the last thing he said for a while.

CHAPTER SIX

SHAPE-SHIFTERS

Captain Krill opened his eyes and stared at a line of metal rivets over his head. Where was he? He got to his feet and took in the bottles, spacesuits, tins and boxes of wing-pong balls stacked around him. He was in the extra-cold store with Rocky, Splash and Fuzz.

"What happened?" he asked, rubbing his eyes with his flippers.

"We were hoping you could tell us that," Rocky said.

"Is my birthday cake OK?" asked Splash.

"You didn't want your birthday cake," Fuzz said.

Splash looked shocked. "Of course I wanted my birthday cake! I chose it, didn't I?"

Rocky shook his head so hard his feathery eyebrows flapped like socks on a windy washing line. "You didn't, Splash. We all saw you eat a pile of space-spinach instead of a piece of cake."

They all started talking at once.

"And then you said the ship needed refuelling—"

"No WAY would I eat space-spinach instead of cake – I'd rather eat my own flippers—"

"ENOUGH!" Captain Krill commanded. "Something weird is going on here and I think I know what. Remember when those pirates attacked us? And there were those four big whooshes? They must have teleported aboard the *Tunafish*."

"You mean, they've beamed their way on to our ship?" said Rocky. "But we haven't seen any extra passengers!"

"That's because *these* pirates are shapeshifters." Captain Krill clasped his flippers behind his back, and paced up and down. "Aliens that take on the shape of other creatures. They're famous for loving space-spinach. They got Splash first. Then Rocky. Then Fuzz. Now they've got me as well."

"You mean when Rocky and Splash started acting weird, it wasn't them at all?" said Fuzz. "It was these shape-shifting things?"

"Exactly," said Captain Krill.

"Thank haddock for that," said Fuzz. "Splash and Rocky's conversation was a lot more boring than usual."

"Hey!" Rocky and Splash said together.

Captain Krill tried the handle of the extra-cold store door. It didn't move.

"We're locked in," he said. "So right now, four aliens that look exactly like us are flying the *Tunafish* towards the extremely rich planet Kroesus."

"What do they want to go there for?" asked Rocky.

"To rob it, of course!" said Splash. "Sometimes I think you have a sprat for a brain, Rocky."

"They're going to pretend to be four

innocent penguin explorers needing fuel," said Captain Krill. "They will get through the security checks and land on Kroesus, then probably shape-shift into Kroesans, turn off the mechanical meteor defence system and bring in that big fleet of black ships to steal everything they can find."

"It'll be the crime of all time!" gasped Fuzz. "And we'll be the suspects!"

"It's our duty to protect the universe and our good name, and stop these villains," said Captain Krill. "One for all…"

"And all for fish!" cried the others, slapping flippers.

The sound echoed around the extra-cold store.

"But we're locked in!" said Rocky. "We can't stop anybody!"

Captain Krill waddled over to a communication button on the wall of the extra-cold store and pressed it. "ICEcube?

Can you hear me?"

"Loud and clear, Captain."

"Can you get us out of here?"

"No. The locks on the doors are controlled by NASA-issue keys only, which are kept in the main cabin."

"So much for your mega-brain, ICEcube," Fuzz grumbled. "What can you tell us about these shape-shifting space-invaders aboard our ship?"

"They are called Dogmutts and they are the most fearsome space pirates in the universe," said ICEcube. "They are cunning, dangerous, determined and unstoppable."

"Nothing stops the Fuzzmeister," said Fuzz, striking a ninja penguin pose.

Captain Krill peered thoughtfully through the storeroom window. "If we can't open the inside door," he said, "we'll have to open the outside one instead."

The Space Penguins stared at the door set in the wall of the extra-cold store. It led to an airlock, which opened out into the inky blackness of space itself.

"I like your thinking, Captain," said Fuzz.

"I don't!" Rocky protested. "He means we go outside and that's proper space out there!"

"It's our only choice." Captain Krill pointed a flipper at the row of spare spacesuits hanging up by the tins of star-whale blubber. "Get yourselves suited up. We're going to spacewalk underneath the *Tunafish* and give those Dogmutts a real birthday surprise!"

CHAPTER SEVEN

SPACEWALK!

The Space Penguins put on the spacesuits and switched on the microphones inside their helmets. They shuffled into the airlock and shut the door that led back into the extra-cold store. Now only one door stood between them and the starry void of space.

"Counting one, two, three," said Captain Krill.

"Very good, Captain," said Rocky. "Four and five come next."

"I'm checking the microphones,

Rocky," said the Captain. "Can everyone hear me?"

Rocky, Fuzz and Splash gave the flippers-up.

"We need to tie ourselves together before we go out there," said the Captain, "otherwise we'll float away."

Floating off alone into space was a horrible thought. The Space Penguins worked quickly, looping a strong piece of steel rope through their space belts and double-checking the knots.

"Ready?" said Captain Krill at last.

"As ready as a guppy in a grillpan," Fuzz said at once. "Time to show those dodgy Dogmutts what the Space Penguins are made of!"

"You are holding on to me, right, Splash?" checked Rocky.

"As tight as a tadpole," Splash promised.

"Tadpoles don't have anything to hold on with!"

"OK, as tight as a trout."

Captain Krill heaved open the great wheel lock on the external door and the Space Penguins stepped out into nothing.

Although penguins are perfect for spacewalking, with their natural abilities in weightless, freezing environments, the enormous darkness made the *Tunafish* crew feel very small and helpless. Space had never looked so spacious. The stars were extra bright, and the silence was deep. Holding firmly to the rope, Captain Krill clanged his magnetic boots against the metal shell of the *Tunafish*. He stuck there like a limpet.

"I'm pleased to say that the boots work," he said into his helmet microphone. "Try and walk quietly, crew. We don't want the Dogmutts to hear us coming. We'll enter through the external airlock door in the freezing-fog room and surprise them in the cabin."

The Space Penguins made a strange sight as they climbed under the belly of the *Tunafish*, hanging upside down like a row of beaky bats. Below them, the stars twinkled and glowed.

"This is so weird," Rocky said happily. "I'm upside down, but I feel like I'm the right way up. It's like swimming in a crazy ocean out here."

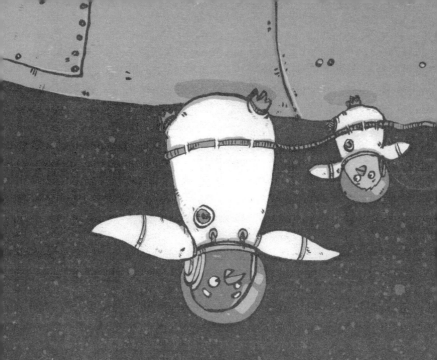

A large planet lay straight ahead of them, with thousands of scary mechanical meteors orbiting it like moons. Kroesus's defence system was hard at work. It looked very unwelcoming, dangerous and too close for comfort. The Space Penguins were running out of time.

Splash's foot suddenly bumped against something. He tugged on the rope to stop everyone else as he stared at the object

beside his feet.

"What have you found, Splash?" asked
the Captain.

Splash plucked the thing from the
underside of the ship and held it up.
It was shaped like a tiny jellyfish, with
metal tentacles and a winking lens.
"I've got no idea," he said, puzzled.

"I think I've seen that before," said
Rocky.

"Let's worry about it when we get back inside," said Fuzz. "We're nearly at the door to the freezing-fog room, guys. We're going to give those Dogmutts a bashing they'll never forget!"

The door opened smoothly, then clicked shut behind the Space Penguins. They gave themselves a couple of minutes in the airlock, getting used to the feeling of gravity again, before opening the door into the freezing-fog room. They were safely back on board.

"That was great," said Rocky, as they wriggled out of their spacesuits and untied themselves. "We should do that more often."

Captain Krill put his flipper on the hatch handle. "Ready?" he asked the others. "GO!"

They burst through the hatch into the cabin, flippers raised. Startled, the invaders jumped out of their seats. There was a moment of frozen silence as the

gmutt penguins and the real penguins
ed at each other.

"That is freaky," said Splash, staring at
Dogmutt Splash.

"I am seriously handsome," said Rocky,
ring at the Dogmutt Rocky and preening
eyebrows.

"This ship needs refuelling," said the
gmutt Captain Krill.

"FIGHT!" shouted Fuzz.

With a whirl of feet and flippers, the
ce Penguins charged at the impostors.

"I've got one!" yelled Rocky.

"Get off me, you winkle-head!" shouted
ash. "I'm the REAL Splash!"

"This ship needs refuelling," said the
gmutt Fuzz.

"You mutant mirror! You dirty
ible!" The real Fuzz leaped on to the
gmutt Fuzz. "I'd never say anything as
ing as that!"

WHAM! BAM! SLAM! As the Space
Penguins rolled and tumbled, wriggled
and wrestled with the Dogmutt invaders
it became harder to tell who was who.
Outside the window, Kroesus's robot
security meteors flared and danced in
the sky.

"This is Kroesus calling," crackled
the communication button. "State your
business. I repeat, state your business."

"This ship needs refuelling," said the Dogmutt Rocky smoothly, fighting off Captain Krill with one flipper.

"Security check one," said the communication button. "Begin weapon scan."

"Wait!" yelled Rocky. "We've been boarded by pirates! Get off me, Splash! Splash? That is you, right?"

"I'm over here!" Splash bawled.

It was getting more and more difficult to see what they were doing. Two Fuzzes, two Rockys, two Splashes, two Captains – eight penguins, flippers flying, feet waddling, bellies bumping. It was like fighting full-length mirrors.

"This is impossible!" shouted Splash, battling as hard as he could.

"This impostor Captain is well strong!" Rocky shouted, fighting Captain Krill.

"I'm not an impostor," yelled the Captain. He pulled hard on Rocky's eyebrows. "I'm the real deal!"

Rocky fought harder. "How do I know you're telling the truth?"

The Space Penguins – or maybe the Dogmutts – were forced backwards.

"Good effort, Splash!" one Splash shouted at the other Splash.

"That's YOU, you feather-brained flounder!" Fuzz pummelled at everything within reach of his tiny flippers. "How can you congratulate yourself?"

"You do it all the time," Rocky panted.

"Not—" WHAM! "when—" POW! "I'm—" CHONK! "fighting—" KLANG! "shape-shifters!"

The Dogmutts – or maybe the Space Penguins – were losing the battle. With one final shove they tumbled down into the wing-pong room. The hatch closed with a CLICK and there was the grating sound of a NASA-issue key turning in the lock.

CHAPTER EIGHT

BURD FLOO

The Space Penguins sat glumly in the wing-pong room.

"That went well," said Rocky.

"No, it didn't," Fuzz said. "With all that penguin confusion in the cabin, we're prisoners again. I'm so mad, I could wrestle a rabid rhinoceros."

Rocky rolled his eyes. "I was joking."

"It's no joking matter!" said Fuzz. "And we haven't even got any wing-pong balls to play with."

Captain Krill stood with one yellow
r-patch pressed to the locked wing-
ng room hatch. "The good news is, the
oesans haven't shut down their meteor
fence system yet," he reported, as he
tened to the Dogmutts in the cabin
ove. "Rocky alerted Kroesus when he
outed out that we had space pirates on
ard. They haven't let us in."

"That's good news?" said Rocky. "We're
ll moving! In half an hour, we'll hit the
oesan atmosphere and burst into fish-
voured flames!"

"There's bad news, too," said the
ptain. "The Dogmutts are planning to fly
rough the meteors and land on Kroesus
yway."

"Impossible!" cried Rocky. "Even I
uldn't do it!"

"Then let us all die as bravely as
rnacles," said Fuzz in a noble voice.

"I'd rather *live* as bravely as a penguin," said Splash. "But first I want to figure out how this ended up on our ship." He waved the jellyfish-like thing he'd plucked off the *Tunafish* during their spacewalk. "It's a camera. I've been checking its memory banks. It's been transmitting information about us ever since we left Beaky Wader's Death Starfish space station three months ago."

"I knew I'd seen it before," Rocky gasped. "I found it on my belt in the Death Starfish space port and flicked it off!"

"Ever since Beaky asked us to live with him on his space station and we turned him down, he's been after us," said Captain Krill. "He must have attached the camera to the *Tunafish*. It explains how he knew where we were that time he attacked us and we crash-landed. And it explains how he found us at the Superchase Space Race. He's been watching us all along!"

"It hasn't helped him much," said Fuzz. "We still wrecked his space station and ruined his chances of winning the Superchase Space Race, not to mention spoiling his special armour and blowing him up a couple of times. I'm guessing Beaky Wader really hates us."

"Aren't we supposed to call him 'Dark' Wader now?" asked Splash. "I know he used to be our space mate aboard the *Tunafish*, but he's the most evil villain in the universe these days."

"I'd sooner give him a collar and lead and call him Bark Wader," said Fuzz.

"Or a lovely singing voice," said Rocky. "Then he'd be Lark Wader."

"Or we could cover him in grass," said Splash, "and make him Park Wader."

"Pull yourselves together, crew," said

Captain Krill, as Rocky, Fuzz and Splash all roared with laughter. "In thirty minutes we'll all be deep-fried penguin puffs. We need a plan."

Splash stopped laughing and straightened his goggles. He waved the jelly-cam in the air. "I have it, Captain," he said. "Let's send Beaky a message he can't resist."

"What sort of message?" asked Captain Krill.

"We'll tell him that the Space Penguins are vulnerable to attack," said Splash. "When he turns up with all guns blazing to blow us out of the sky, the Dogmutts will have to turn away from the flaming meteors in order to fight him off."

"There's a flaw in that plan somewhere," said the Captain. "But I can't put my flipper on it."

"It'll be easy-peasy – like taking

doughnuts from a dolphin," said Fuzz happily. "If dolphins liked doughnuts."

"Thirty minutes until impact," said ICEcube.

"Flaw or no flaw, it's the only plan we have," Captain Krill said, making a decision. "Send the message, Splash."

Several million light years away, a shiny silver Squid-G spacecraft was cruising along through the vastness of space. It looked like a tiny silver bug floating on an enormous black ocean. A large armour-plated penguin hungrily scanned the skies through the windscreen.

"Where are they, Crabba?" hissed Dark Wader. "Find those Space Penguins for me. I will thread them on to a stick and barbecue them. I will use their beaks as cutlery handles. I will pull out their feathers one by one and make them dance the tango on a bed of hot coals! Revenge will be MINE!"

"You've been saying that for weeks, boss," said the small scaly alien sitting on Dark Wader's shoulder. "Let's admit that we've lost them and all go home."

"NEVER!" roared Dark Wader. "They blew me up, Crabba!"

"You blew yourself up," Crabba pointed out. "It was your mine on the Superchase Space Race finishing line."

"If you don't shut up," said Dark Wader, "I'll barbecue *you* instead."

Another spacecraft flew level with
ark Wader's Squid-G. It was bright red
nd twinkled with jewels. At the helm
as an angry-looking pig-shaped alien
ith heavy jewels in his butterfly-like
ars.

Dark Wader pressed a button on
he control panel. "What about you,
kyporker?" he growled down the
ntercom at the red spaceship. "Have you
en those penguins yet? I'm going to blow

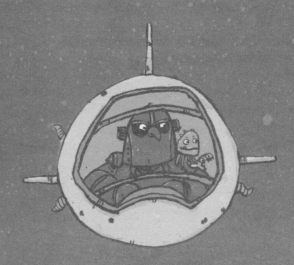

them up like fish-flavoured bubblegum."

"IF I SEE THOSE BLACK AND WHITE BANDITS I'LL BLOW THEM UP MYSELF!" screamed Anadin Skyporker, revving his red spacecraft a little faster. Anadin Skyporker, Emperor of the planet Sossij, hated the Space Penguins almost as much as Dark Wader did. "NO ONE STOPS ME FROM WINNING MY SUPERCHASE SPACE RACE AND GETS AWAY WITH IT!"

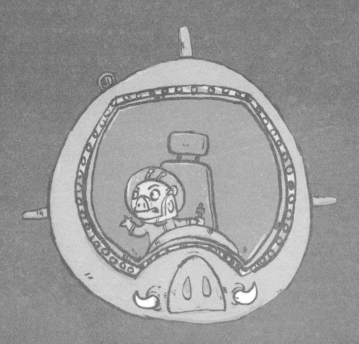

One of the control-panel screens started blinking.

"Message coming through from our jelly-cam on-board the *Tunafish*," said Crabba, sitting up straight. "We must finally be in range."

"At last!" Dark Wader gasped. "What does it say?"

SPACE PENGUINS HEADING TOWARDS PLANET KROESUS IN SECTION L OF THE UNIVERSE. CREW VULNERABLE TO ATTACK. REVENGE NOW OR NEVER.

Dark Wader thumped the control panel with delight. A couple of buttons fell off with a clunk. "We've got them, Crabba! Ask your jelly-cam why they're so vulnerable."

Crabba scuttled to the control panel and typed in the question.

WHY VULNERABLE?

There was a pause. An answer winked

up: BURD FLOO.

Dark Wader laughed with glee. "That's not something I have to worry about. Not now I'm a pengbot. We have them like eggs in a frying pan!"

Crabba frowned. "I don't think that's how you spell 'bird flu', boss."

"So what? Spelling never changed anything. Send for our entire Squid-G fighting force and set the coordinates for Section L immediately!"

"I'm summoning squadrons of X-jets from Sossij, too!" Anadin Skyporker screeched down the intercom. "We'll fillet them like flounders. We'll smoke them like kippers. Wait for me!"

CHAPTER NINE

FIGHT, FIGHT, FIGHT

"I hope I spelled 'bird flu' right," Splash said.

"Let us know the minute you see any Squid-Gs, ICEcube," said Captain Krill.

A huge meteor rocketed past the wing-pong-room window. With a great BANG it burst into flames.

"This is the end," groaned Rocky.

"Disturbance in the space-time continuum, Captain," said ICEcube, as two more mechanical meteors exploded nearby. BANG! BANG! "A fleet of Squid-G fighters and X-jets just leaped ten million light years to join us."

"The message worked!" cheered Splash. "Dark Wader's on his way! The Dogmutts will have to turn back to fight him off. I'm a genius!"

"Did you say Squid-Gs and *X-jets*, ICEcube?" said Captain Krill. "X-jets, as in the Emperor of Sossij's elite space-fighters?"

"Affirmative, Captain."

"How many?"

"Sixty-two," said ICEcube. "Plus thirty-eight Squid-Gs."

"I've found the flaw in our plan," said Captain Krill. "It's not just the Dogmutts aboard the *Tunafish*. It's *us*, too! And now Skyporker's helping Dark Wader, we have a hundred spaceships all wanting to blow us up."

The Space Penguins stared at each
her. It *was* a problem.

PYOW! PYOW!

PYOW! PYOW! PYOW!

"Beaky's space guns!" Rocky gasped.

"We need to take matters into our own
ppers," said Captain Krill, peering out
rough the wing-pong-room window.
We can't wait for Wader and Skyporker
finish us off."

"Then let's go," said Splash.

"We're locked in," Captain Krill
minded his ship's engineer.

"Duh," said Fuzz.

The Ship's Engineer waddled to a small
pboard and took out a silver key on a
ring marked WING-PONG ROOM SPARE
EY.

"Is that what I think it is?" said Rocky
amazement, as Splash fitted it into the
ck.

"I've kept the NASA-issue spare key in here ever since the Captain beat Beaky at wing-pong and Beaky locked him in for revenge," Splash explained, turning the key.

"You mean, we could have got out of here ages ago?" demanded Fuzz. "Why didn't you say something?"

"It wasn't necessary," Splash said. "Now, it is."

The hatch opened with a gentle click.

The Space Penguins peered out.

"YOU DO NOT HAVE PERMISSION TO ENTER THE KROESAN ATMOSPHERE," boomed the intercom. "TURN BACK OR PREPARE TO DIE."

"What a lovely welcome," said Fuzz. "Penguin power!"

He leaped at the Dogmutt Fuzz, flippers at the ready. CLONK!

"I almost feel bad about that," he added as the Dogmutt penguin keeled over and hit the floor beak first. "He was a lot smaller than me."

"He's exactly the same as you, Fuzz," said Rocky, karate-chopping his Dogmutt double's flippers away from the control panel. "That's the point."

CHONK! CLUNK! THUNK!

"No way am I that small!" Fuzz insisted, as he leaped through the air feet first, sending the Dogmutt Captain flying.

"Keep talking, crew!" shouted Captain Krill. He was fighting hard with the Dogmutt Splash. "These guys only have about three things to say! That's how we'll know who's fighting who!"

"What's the capital of Norway?" asked Splash.

"This ship needs refuelling," said the Dogmutt Captain.

"Wrong answer!" shouted Splash, and stomped on the Dogmutt Captain's webbed feet.

"*I* didn't know that one, Splash," said Captain Krill, his feet and flippers a blur. "Try something easier next time. Take THAT, you dog-faced dogfish!"

"Space-spinach is the worst stuff ever!" shouted Fuzz, as he flew at the Dogmutt Splash, knocking him out with a single ninja chop.

"Check," said the Dogmutt Splash, just before he slid to the floor.

"Splash?" Fuzz prodded the unconscious penguin at his feet. "That's not you, is it?"

"I'm over here!" The real Splash was now engaged in flipper-to-flipper combat with the Dogmutt Rocky.

"Phew," said Fuzz. "That 'check' thing could have gone either way."

PYOW! PYOW! BANG-SPLAT!

Dogmutt Fuzz got back on his feet.

"What is that stink?" gasped Captain Krill, as he danced out of his way.

"A swill-gun cannonball from a
sijan X-jet," Rocky panted back.
They were well and truly in the
esan meteor field now. Huge flaming
ks were hurtling past the windscreen.
t swill guns shook the air. The smell
urning pig-swill was terrible.

"Open the waste-disposal chute, Captain!" Fuzz shouted, shoving the Dogmutt Fuzz hard in the belly. "Bye-by barnacle-brains!"

The Dogmutt's penguin shape dissolv leaving nothing but a smoky dog-shaped figure that floated down the waste-dispos chute.

"Right on target!" Splash shouted. H heaved the Dogmutt Splash up and pusl him between his feathered shoulders. "You next, my goggled friend!"

CLONK! A second smoky-looking Dogmutt ricocheted off the chute walls and vanished. BANG!

"It's been a pleasure knowing me," s Captain Krill, as he pushed the Dogmut Captain briskly into the waste chute.

Dogmutt Rocky swiftly followed. The Space Penguins just glimpsed his pengui feet turning back into smoky paws as the

Captain shut the door. CLANG. Then Rocky
turned a wheel on the wall, opening the
airlock and sending the Dogmutts into the
great black nothing beyond.

"The *Tunafish* suddenly feels rather spacious," said Rocky, gazing at the cabin and the winking flight instruments.

PYOW! PYOW! BANG-SPLAT! PYOW!

"Can we go now, Rocky?" said Captain Krill, as flaming meteors whizzed past the windows and the *Tunafish* juddered and shook in the heart of the battle.

"I'll do my best, Captain!" Rocky leaped into his pilot's chair. "Seatbelts on, everyone. Let's get the hecky-peck out of here, to a bit of empty space where we can hit warp speed."

"Fly like you've never flown before, Rocky!" screamed Fuzz, hopping up and down in his seat.

"I'd prefer it if Rocky flew like he HAD flown before," said Splash. "Like, lots of times and really brilliantly."

The Space Penguins gripped their seats as the *Tunafish* sprang upwards like

a trout leaping for a mayfly. A hundred
Squid-G space guns and X-jet swill guns
swivelled to follow the little spaceship.

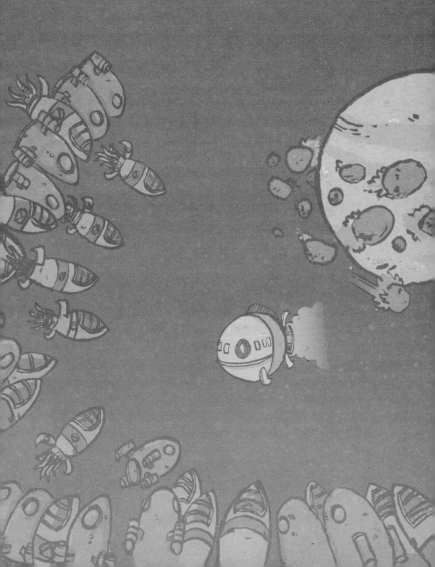

BANG-SPLAT! PYOW!

Rocky made an impossible move, weaving through a wall of gunfire like a shadow, then shot a space cannonball into a swill-gun cannonball with an explosive squelch.

"Wahoo!" roared Fuzz.

Rocky nipped and whizzed and spun through the smoke. Nothing touched him. Nothing came close.

"Nearly there, Rocky," said Captain Krill. "One more burst of speed should do it."

"I'm the King of the Cosmos!" Rocky shouted, as the *Tunafish* jetted free from Kroesus's fiery meteors, the X-jets and the Squid-Gs in a fish-shaped blur. "Warp speed … away!"

And BOOM. They were gone.

P.S.

"Where did they go?" gasped Dark Wade

He peered out of the Squid-G windscreen. The sky was full of burning meteors, but no fish-shaped spaceship could be seen. Squid-Gs and X-jets were flying around like mosquitoes with no o left to bite.

"The *Tunafish* was right there," squealed Anadin Skyporker down the intercom. "I was about to swill it out of the sky!"

"I think they warped out of here," sa Crabba.

"Impossible!" shouted Dark Wader. "The jelly-cam said they were ill! You ca fly a spaceship like that when you're ill!"

Crabba clicked his claws nervously. "I told you 'bird flu' was spelled wrong, boss. The penguins must have found the jelly-cam and sent us a fake message.

They tricked us. Again! I'm off to hide somewhere so you can't barbecue me."

"NO!" Dark Wader yelled, as Crabba scuttled away. "Skyporker, do something!"

"YOU do something!" Anadin Skyporker screamed back.

"How about I blow YOU up instead?" Dark Wader growled.

"Not if I blow YOU up first!"

The Sossij emperor swivelled his guns to point at Dark Wader. Dark Wader swivelled his guns to point at the Sossij emperor.

"I knew this was going to end badly," said Crabba, clambering back on to Dark Wader's shoulder to get a better look.

"Ready," hissed Skyporker.

"Aim," snarled Dark Wader.

There was a pause.

"Hey, you there!" The Sossij emperor suddenly sounded shocked. "Weird smoky guy! What are you doing on my ship? Why is it so cold in here?"

"I was about to ask the same thing," said the pengbot, his laser eyes brightening with surprise at the dog-shaped visitor who had silently appeared in the Squid-G cabin.

"Oh, poo…"

"Destination: planet Kroesus," said the Dogmutt Dark Wader, settling into the controls. "Estimated duration of flight: eight minutes. Estimated time of arrival: twenty-five hundred hours, Kroesus time."

SPACE PENGUINS

The intercom crackled.

"Check," the Dogmutt Anadin
Skyporker replied.

Take a peek at the Space Penguins'
first adventure:

STAR ATTACK!

LOADING...

LOADING...

LOADING...

Welcome aboard the spaceship *Tunafish*. This is your Intergalactic Computer Engine speaking. You can call me ICEcube for short.

I'm here to guide the *Tunafish* through the universe, scan the galaxy for meteor storms and spot any black holes. My penguin crew would have flapped their last flap years ago if it wasn't for me.

Penguin crew? Yup! Penguins are perfect for space missions. They're good at swimming (being in space is a lot like swimming), cheap to train, and untroubled by temperatures of near zero.

But why are these penguins in space? You'll have to ask NASA about that. Their finest scientists started a top-secret mission to send penguins further and faster than any creature had gone before. They designed the spaceship *Tunafish* for all their needs. But the spaceship disappeared. Everyone thought that the mission had simply been a failure. Little did they know that the *Tunafish* and its penguin crew had just been sucked through a wormhole into Deep Space.

My database suggests that the best word for this is: whoops!

So now these penguins are travelling in search of a nice planet to call home. In the course of their quest, they've become intergalactic heroes. They've saved the cat race of Miaow from certain death on the planet Woofbark. They've even destroyed a large pair of frozen pants that was endangering space traffic on the tiny planet of Bum. This is mostly down to me, of course. Impressed?

There were five penguins to begin with, but the first mate, Beaky Wader, disappeared from the *Tunafish* three years ago after a nasty argument about who was going to be Captain. The words, "You haven't seen the last of me," echoed around the spaceship for days. Good riddance, I say. Beaky Wader was Trouble with a capital Fish.

And now – well, now they're still looking for the perfect penguin planet. We'll probably be rescuing things as we go along, so I know you're as excited as I am to be here. Fasten your seat belt and have a sardine. I would say that you are in safe hands, but penguins only have flippers.

Five. Four. Three. Two. One…

CHAPTER ONE

BOBBY CHEESE HAS A BAD DAY

"HELP!" bawled Bobby Cheese, commander of intergalactic pizza-delivery spaceship, the *Doughball*, as he zoomed towards certain death.

A crazy-looking spacecraft had appeared out of nowhere, driving him off-course in a blaze of gunfire.

"Awaiting instruction," said the *Doughball*'s computer.

"I AM instructing you!" yelled Bobby Cheese. "HELP me!"

He thumped all the buttons on the
Doughball's juddering control panel in
a panic. Bobby Cheese was a six-armed
alien from the planet Bo-Ki, but even so,
two thousand buttons took a long time to
thump.

"Awaiting instruction," said the
computer again. "Chill out, Cheese," it
added.

"Don't tell me to chill out!" Bobby
Cheese wailed. "We're hopelessly out
of control!"

Stars shot past the *Doughball*'s
windows at weird angles. Bobby Cheese
moaned. He didn't know if he was upside
down or the right way up.

"Awaiting instruction," said the
computer for the third time.

"You're useless!" cried Bobby Cheese.
"We've got nearly a thousand pizzas flying
around in the back. They'll be ruined.

We'll be picking mozzarella out of the fuselage for weeks unless we get this craft back under control!"

"We'll be picking you out of the fuselage as well," the computer said helpfully.

"Quit the small talk and get me out here. Have you any idea who's attacking us?" Bobby Cheese yelled.

The computer was quiet for a second. "The attack is by Squid-G fighters," it said at last.

"Squidgy what?"

"Squid-G fighters. Spacecrafts with considerable firepower and a strong smell of fish."

"But why are they attacking me?" shrieked Bobby Cheese.

"For fun?" suggested the computer.

The *Doughball* spun faster. Its nose dipped further. The stars outside grew

wonkier. Bobby Cheese glanced at a tattered poster stuck on the wall. The poster showed four penguins posing beside a fish-shaped spacecraft.

"Only the heroic astronauts of the *Tunafish* can help me now," he gasped. "We have to contact them!"

"But they're just penguins," said the computer. "Are you sure you want to put your life into the flippers of four flightless birds?"

"They're not just penguins!" cried Bobby Cheese. "They're space-fighting heroes! If I haven't died by the time they get here, remind me to get their autographs!"

The wonky stars suddenly disappeared from view altogether as the spinning *Doughball* plunged into a bank of mist. Bobby Cheese typed a shaky distress call to the spaceship *Tunafish* and

ressed SEND. Squinting desperately
through the windscreen, his eyes widened
the sight of a gigantic five-pointed star
ooming ahead of him.

"What's that? Is it a planet?"

"Planets don't have pointy bits. That's
space station," reported the computer.

The air filled with a humming sound.
obby Cheese groaned and pressed his
ands to as many of his ears as he could
each. It was over. The *Doughball* was
uffed.

Where was the *Tunafish* in his hour
f greatest need?